For Deek – L.G.
For Mum and Dad – J.M

This book belongs to

_____

The artwork in this book was created using Indian ink, gouache and digital media

First published in 2021 by Floris Books. Text © 2021 Louise Greig. Illustrations © 2021 Júlia Moscardó
Louise Greig and Júlia Moscardó assert their right under the Copyright, Designs and Patents Act 1988 to be recognised as the
Author and Illustrator of this Work. All rights reserved. No part of this book may be reproduced without prior permission of
Floris Books, Edinburgh www.florisbooks.co.uk British Library CIP Data available
ISBN 978-178250-713-0 Printed in Malaysia by Tien Wah Press

FSC
www.fsc.org
MIX
Paper from
responsible sources
FSC® C012700

Floris Books supports sustainable forest management
by printing this book on materials made from wood that
comes from responsible sources and reclaimed material

Home of the Wild

Louise Greig and Júlia Moscardó

Floris
Books

There is a boy who breathes the wild,
who knows every rustle in the circling pines,
who hears the sweep of every wing,
and the quietest heartbeat on the wind.

There is a boy who has mended tails
and patched up wings,
who has tended, nursed
and fed small things.
Inside a house, safe and warm,
a welcome shelter from any storm.

There is a boy who knows
when a tiny bundle of dappled leaves
is not what it seems,
but a trembling creature in the breaking dawn.
Its mother gone. All alone.
He whispers into soft velvet,
"I'll carry you home."

And he does.
Back to a warm room,
where his mother smiles but gently warns,
"She can stay till she is strong,
but the wild is where fawns belong.
A house is not a home for wild things;
wild things need to run, and soar, and swim."

The boy nods,
and on his lips a name comes:
"Alba."

Alba sleeps. Alba stands. Alba leans.
The boy never leaves her side.
Until – on legs as thin as rose stems – Alba runs.

They leap and chase over burn and heather.
Always together.

His mother, looking on,
sees the growing bond between a boy and a fawn.
But she knows:
soon Alba will be strong.

Summer is here. The days are long.
Green fills the grass and the lush leaves.
Alba's sunlit coat gleams,
and her dark eyes glitter like the dancing streams.

Beneath the trees,
side by side,
two shadows join.
One fawn. One boy.

Then come words that bring an end to the joy:
"Alba must leave now she is strong,
for the wild is where fawns belong.
A house is not a home for wild things;
wild things need to run, and soar, and swim."

The boy sits silent, alone as the moon.
The tall pines sway,
the foxgloves bloom,
the waterfall tinkles a sweet tune,
the thrush sings her song.

But nothing is the same with Alba gone.

The day turns dark. The air shivers.
A scudding cloud shudders, bringing thunder.

The boy looks up at angry skies.
"Alba! Where are you?" he cries.
He must find her,
for he knows roaring storms
do not care about gentle fawns.

But tracks in the rain all look the same.
He stumbles over bracken and lichen,
over tree roots and moss.
Soon the boy is lost.
"Help!" Fear floods his voice.
"Help!"
Can anyone hear his calls?

There is a fawn who breathes the wild,
who is learning every rustle in the circling pines,
who hears the beat of rain-soaked wings,
and a boy's faint cry on the booming wind.

There is a fawn wild and strong,
who leaps,
from fallen tree to slippery stone,
who finds a boy, afraid, alone.
They huddle together,
two shapes joined.
One boy. One fawn.

The raging clouds move on.
The sullen air clears.
Out comes the brightening yellow sun.

Alba and the boy run.
Through a forest that makes sense again,
to a familiar house, in a familiar glen,
where a boy calls,
"Mother, Alba found me in the storm!"
And a mother's worried heart lifts, and warms.

Now the boy knows his fawn is strong.
Into soft ears he whispers,
"Go now, Alba,
for the wild is where fawns like you belong."

There is a boy.
There is a fawn.
They breathe the wild.
They know every rustle in the circling pines.
They hear the sweep of every wing.

And forever, yes forever,
they will hear each other's heartbeat on the wind.

About the author and illustrator

Louise Greig is an award-winning poet and author from Scotland. Her picture books, many inspired by the Scottish landscape and the company of animals, include *The Night Box* and *The Island and the Bear*. *The Night Box* made the shortlist for the Waterstones Children's Book Prize and was nominated for the Kate Greenaway Medal. Louise lives in Aberdeen, north-east Scotland, with her husband.

Júlia Moscardó is an illustrator and painter from Spain. She studied Fine Art in València, and Children's Book Illustration at the Cambridge School of Art. She currently lives in Nottingham, England. *Home of the Wild* is her first picture book.